DERMOT BOLGER

In High Germany

Born in Dublin in 1959, Dermot Bolger is
a novelist, poet and playwright.
His seven novels include *The Journey
Home*, *Father's Music* and *The Temptation*
(which is being published in 2000). His
plays include *The Lament for Arthur
Cleary* and *April Bright*. He also devised
the best-selling collaborative novels,
Finbar's Hotel and *Ladies' Night at
Finbar's Hotel*.

IN HIGH GERMANY
This version first published in Ireland in October 1999
by New Island Books,
2 Brookside,
Dundrum Road,
Dublin 14

1 3 5 7 9 10 8 6 4 2

A CIP catalogue record for this book is available from the British Library

ISBN 1 902602 14 5

The Arts Council
An Chomhairle Ealaíon

**New Island Books receives financial assistance from The Arts Council
(An Chomhairle Ealaíon), Dublin, Ireland.**

This text of *In High Germany* is a specially abridged and revised version of the
author's stage play of the same name, first performed by the Gate Theatre, Dublin.
This text is not for public performance. The performance text is available in *Dermot
Bolger: Plays 1* (published by Methuen in the UK and New Island in Ireland, 2000).
No performance may be staged unless a licence is obtained in advance from the
author's agents, Curtis Brown, 4th floor, Haymarket House, 28/29 Haymarket,
London SW1Y 4SP.
All poems at the end of the book (except 'Approaching Forty') are taken from
Taking My Letters Back: New and Selected Poems by Dermot Bolger (New Island,
1998) and are reproduced here by permission of the author.

Typeset by New Island Books
Printed by Cox & Wyman, Reading, Berks.
Cover design by Artmark

THE OPEN DOOR SERIES is a new experience in reading. Consisting of six original or adapted works from some of Ireland's best-loved authors, these short novels are ideal for improving your reading skills while at the same time enjoying all the benefits of a good story. There's something to suit everyone's taste in this unique series, with themes of love — lost, found and forbidden — of family strife, of the thrills of supporting the Irish soccer team, of emigration, or of being a Private Eye on Dublin's mean streets. And, like all good stories, we hope these books will open doors — of the imagination and of opportunity — for adult readers of all ages.

Royalties from the Irish sales of the Open Door series will go to a charity of the author's choice.

ALSO IN THE SERIES

The Open Door series is developed with the assistance of the City of Dublin Vocational Education Committee and Bank of Ireland.

Dear Reader,

On behalf of myself and the other contributing authors, I would like to welcome you to the Open Door series. We hope that you enjoy the novels and that reading becomes a lasting pleasure in your life.

Warmest wishes,

Patricia Scanlan.

Patricia Scanlan
Series Editor

CONTENTS

IN HIGH GERMANY

GLOSSARY

Suas, seas, suas, seas: Up, down, up, down.

Liathróid, a Mháistir: A ball, Sir.

Cafollas: A family with lots of fish and chip shops in Dublin.

Reeperbahn: The red light area of Hamburg.

Gelsenkirchen: The town where Ireland played Holland in 1988.

You are eleven now, Son. All you think of every day is football, football and more football. Upsetting the old man in the flat below us by kicking ball on the grass, in the car park spaces. Anywhere you can find room in this apartment block.

How very un-German of you not to obey the house rule about making noise. The afternoon hours when one is not allowed to use the Hoover or play the radio too loud. Their neat German laws. It was never like that at home in Dublin, with kids shouting night and day. But Dublin will never be your home and it is no longer mine.

I am Irish in Germany. You are half-Irish in Germany and half-German in Ireland. Maybe it is even harder for you than for me, in no man's land. Your German accent and your Irish looks. When you grow up, perhaps you will play football for some big German team. But if you ever become a star, I will make sure that the football shirt you wear will be the green one of Ireland.

That was the shirt I was wearing twelve years ago, when I first heard, in a phone call, that you were going to be born. Sometimes now you ask me about that. About the last time I saw Ireland play. Not in Dublin, but here in Germany, when I followed them around in Euro 1988. I saw them play England and Russia and Holland.

That was the last week of my youth or at least of my old life. The last time I stood among lots of Irish voices. The last day I woke without thinking of myself in a new way — as a father.

Some nights still, when I am getting a train in the main station, I remember that night back in 1988. Holland had just beaten Ireland. I came back here to Hamburg without phoning your mother to tell her I was coming.

It was late at night. The station was empty when the train got in from the town where the Dutch game had been played.

I remember the cold light on the platform. I sat down on a bench. I threw my bag and sleeping bag on the ground. I lit cigarette after cigarette, kicking an old can with my feet. I was still wearing my Irish shirt and scarf. But it took me two hours of sitting there before I was able to leave my old life behind. Before I went home to face your mother (or my girl friend, as she was then), knowing that you were growing inside her.

♣

I still wake up at night, reliving that day. Wishing we could have hung on for a draw against Holland and made it into the semi-finals of Euro '88. I remember how the road into the football ground was paved with loose stones. There were almost as many loose stones as there were Dutch skinheads to throw them at us if Holland lost.

I thought about the stones a lot during that match, when I could think of anything at all. Sweating with the heat. Sweating with the fear. My throat raw from shouting. My hands raised, calling:

"*Ireland! Ireland! Ireland!*"

How would we ever get out of that ground alive? Away from the Dutch skinheads if Ireland held on for a draw? But really I didn't care how we got away. I would have faced every rock if we could have hung on for the draw. If I could have come back to Hamburg that night, not alone after losing, but bringing my old friends here for the semi-final to be played in this city.

If I could only have arrived at the train station that night with Shane and Mick and still felt that I was part of my old life with my old friends.

The only way to reach the ground for the Dutch game was to take these tiny trains. More like trams really. With only room for maybe forty people, packed up tight.

Around fifty of us packed into one, on the street where we had been drinking the local beer. We took off for the game. The first stop was fine. No one got on and no one got off. The second stop was the problem. There were sixty of them. Dutch skinheads. The real McCoy. These boys were mean bastards. Bald heads painted orange. Boots as thick as the walls of Limerick jail. Sticks in their fists. Eyes like hard sweets from Bray that would break your teeth.

They didn't all get in. Just as many as would fit between us and the roof. One of them had his face pressed against mine. He had been drinking. I looked at him in fear, then did what every Irish man does when in doubt abroad. I raised my fist in the air and slagged the Brits.

"If you hate the Queen of England clap your hands,

If you hate the Queen of England clap your hands,
If you hate the Queen of England,
Hate the Queen of England,
If you hate the Queen of England clap your
*   hands."*

The Dutch skinheads smiled, banged their sticks on the roof and sang along. Would we ever get to the football ground? The train stopping and starting. Nobody getting on or off. Every Irishman trying to think of new songs to keep the skinheads happy.

"The Queen Mother is a man, do-da, do-da
The Queen Mother is a man, do-da, do-da, day."

"Yes, do-da-do-da day!" said the Dutch skinhead beside me. He took out a cigarette and asked me for a light.

I took out a cigarette lighter from my pocket and began to raise it. Then I remembered. I had two cigarette lighters. A plain white one and another I had found in a bar after the England game a few days before, with a big Union Jack on the side. I closed my eyes, held the lighter up and flicked it.

No thump in the face came. I opened my eyes. The lighter was snow white. And they say there is no God, eh?

♣

You often ask me why I love to hang around train stations. What I find so interesting in them. You see, growing up in Germany, Son, you would not know how different it is from Dublin and from Ireland when I was your age.

Trains have no magic for you. You cross Hamburg in them easily. Without thinking. You know the web of stations. Where to change trains to get anywhere. Back then in Ireland it was so different.

I have always had a dream about making a film set in a railway station. It would star a secret agent from some small country.

The film opens with him going to an empty flat in Russia to rob secret papers. He gets hit over the head. The picture goes into darkness. Followed by a blur of railway tracks until, all of a sudden, he wakes up.

OK, he knows he is in a railway station waiting room. But where? That is the question. There is just silence. Nobody is about. The glow of dawn at the tiny window above the wooden seat. Could he be in France? The USA? New Zealand? Finland? Cuba? Are there armed police outside? A dead blonde on the platform. Naked except for a fur coat and a tattoo on her bottom.

He jumps up onto the seat. Throws the window open. Puts his head out and sees them ... sheep! Nothing but sheep. Sheep, sheep and more sheep! The camera moves back to show the sign over his head for LIMERICK JUNCTION!

Limerick Junction. That was how I always saw train stations. Old buildings hidden at the back end of small towns. One train in the morning. One train at night. Miss it and you were stranded.

And, don't ask me how, but even if you were only going from Dublin to Drogheda you still always found yourself sitting on your backside for two hours in Limerick Junction.

We saw every station on Sunday mornings when I was growing up. On our way to Cork, Limerick, Dundalk, Athlone, Sligo. Once, after Waterford beat Bohemians, the team bus broke down. The whole team had to come back on the train with us.

"What are you doing here?" one of the fans shouted at the manager in the queue.

"I'm getting a train ticket for the team."

"You'll be doing well," the fan told him. "They're not worth the price of one!"

♣

Every station was the same. Sleepy porters in big hats shuffling out with a flag to wave the train on. Scratching their backsides at the same time. And always the rusty metal bridge. The name of the town laid out in white stones in a flower bed. The platform like a ghost town until ten minutes before the train was due. We would hang around the platform to watch the young Civil Servants and Library Assistants, who had come home for the weekend. They were being sent back to bedsit-land in Dublin by Mammy and Daddy, with clean underwear in their bags.

Not that we always had it so easy, mind you. Limerick was a hole. Athlone the same. Every local thug and skinhead wanting to prove they were as tough as the skinheads in Dublin by trying to kick our heads in.

"Welcome to the Irish countryside," Shane would say, as we ran down back lanes for our lives. "They are just letting us know how glad they are to see us!"

It's funny, Son, the way train stations always interest me. Maybe it is because of all the old photos. My mother had lots of them in an old biscuit tin at home. Meeting Daddy off the train at Westland Row. Seeing Daddy back onto the train at Westland Row.

How many times were passers-by asked to snap them standing on that platform. Awkward together in public like any Irish husband and wife? Not hugging or anything. Always with a little space left between them? That little space shrunk and grew in Westland Row. The train wheels bringing him back to England, chanting over and over ...

"You will never go back, you will never go back!"

Black '57. That was the year when the building game collapsed in Ireland. All the jobs suddenly gone. I was one year of age. A tiny bundle of love. Daddy was a shadow coming and going, from London and York and Leeds. The postman bringing a registered letter with crisp English banknotes every Friday. Daddy was a black travel bag carried in and out of Westland Row every few months. Bottles of Guinness for him and a Babysham for my mother on the night before he went back across the water. And always he would sing the same song:

"And still I live in hope to see, The Holy Ground once more."

It would have been so much easier for him, I know, to have just picked up his one-year-old bundle of love and left through Westland Row for a new life in England. All his brothers and sisters already had. But Da refused to. He had guts, my da. I'd say that for him. Guts and dreams.

Dreams that I would grow up under an Irish flag, knowing that I belonged somewhere. A free person in a free land. Not that he would have said it that way, or any way, for that matter. He didn't speak much, my da. Just worked till he dropped dead a few weeks after the US factory gave him the brush-off in 1983.

♣

My mother and father's stories were like the best old films. They always began and ended in railways stations. So does the story of that last week I spent with my friends following the Irish team in Germany in 1988. Mick and Shane and me. But not Limerick Junction.

Real stations this time, or at least big train stations. Hamburg and Essen. Hamburg in hope, the day before the England match. Essen in farewell after the Dutch one. Not places that we ever dreamt we would wind up in when we first met, Mick and Shane and me. All of us five years of age with short pants. Off to school for the first time. Pissing ourselves with fright. I think Mick spoke for the first time when we were seven. It was also the first time Shane paused for breath. Shane was small and hard, with the same waddle as a duck as he lunged in after the ball. He got more kicks off other kids than he ever got at that ball.

Captain Shane we called him, or, as he said himself, "Captain Shane Birds-Eye and his cod pieces."

It took me ten years to get the joke. Mick said that he figured it out when he was six, but he just never got around to laughing. He never got around to saying anything. Our teacher, O'Brien, could ask him a question, hop up on the desk with canes, whips and daggers. Mick would just look back at him with the same stupid stare.

O'Brien never hit him. He would turn away in defeat and make some remark about planting Mick with the other vegetables in the fields. But as soon as O'Brien's back was turned, without even looking down, Mick would mutter the right answer to me. Mick knew everything except his letters. He just couldn't seem to write things down.

How could I even start to tell you about that school yard in Dublin, Son? It was like something from a hundred years ago. A big row of cement slabs. Weeds growing between them. Seagulls flying overhead as we were marched into lines at the end of break.

O'Brien, our teacher, would stand on the top step. Bark out orders in Irish. Telling us to lift our hands to touch the shoulder of the boy in front and then to drop them again.

"*Suas, seas, suas, seas.*"

O'Brien always watched over us, with a strap in his hand like it was part of him. Maybe he slept at night with it still in his fist.

A long wooden bench ran all the way down the shed where we sat to eat. Talking. Joking. Laughing. Eating lunch quickly. Waiting to get out there on the concrete, among the litter of bread and papers. Sandals. Boots. Shoes. Runners. Kicking out, rushing after that one dirty plastic football.

Forty forwards with no backs or goalkeepers. Coats piled up as goalposts. And there we would be, Shane and Mick and me, in the thick of it. Kicking, shoving, together, united. Till we were caught by the blast of O'Brien's whistle.

"*Suas, seas, suas, seas…*"

Touch the shoulder of the boy in front of you in the line. Look at his short hair. Watch out for O'Brien pacing behind. With your legs still tingling.

Your breath still panting from that game. Your feet itching for the last, perfect kick, to score in your head the cup-winning goal for Bohs.

Instead, O'Brien took us down the field and stood us in front of a ball.

"This is a ball! A what, boy?" he shouted at me.

"A ball, sir," I replied.

"In Irish!" he shouted.

"*Liathróid, a Mháistir.*"

"And what do you do with it, boy?"

"Kick it, sir."

"And what else, boy?"

"Head it, sir?"

He roared at us then. "You pick it up, boy! Pick it up! Pick it up! Pick it up!"

I reached for it and he screamed:

"Not off the ground! Use your foot. Use your foot off the ground, boy! Do you not know the first rule of Gaelic? Now run with it. Not more than four steps at a time. Solo it! Solo it! Solo it! Solo it!"

We ran over the grass, trying to bounce the ball and solo it. Forced to play a game that felt foreign to us, until O'Brien finally screamed at me in fury:

"What arse end of the bog are you from at all, boy?"

"The street, sir, the city street."

He had a small problem with Mick and Shane and me. O'Brien could not accept that we lived with other hopes and dreams to his. The notes in his teacher-training book did not include the likes of us — or city streets or soccer.

"A Brit sport. An English game played only by Englishmen," he would scream, if any of us dared to speak of an English football team. Or were seen heading a football on the street outside the school. Soccer was like something evil and un-Irish. It had to be stamped out of our lives. O'Brien, with his strap, felt that he was the man to do it.

Not that it mattered much. He was on the way out, O'Brien. This is 1966 I am talking about. Things were looking up for Ireland by then. Sean Lamass was playing poker at night over Cafollas' chip-shop in O'Connell Street. Westland Row had been renamed Pearse Street Station. And we clapped hands till Daddy came home from England for the last time.

The new US factory with the gold sign over the gate was where Daddy was heading. His new blue uniform. The odd feel of him coming home for his tea every evening. His travel bag hung from a nail in the shed where he took out his spade. He joined with all the other country voices calling to each other across hedges in the long back gardens.

"Call them spuds, eh? It's the Kerr's Pinks you want."

All the men on my street were up from Galway, Mayo and Kerry. They lived for the country Gaelic scores and The Walton's music radio programme.

"And remember if you feel like singing, do sing an Irish song."

In school O'Brien was marching us up and down the yard behind a 1798 pike. He made us try on skirts to take part in the 1916 show in Croke Park. RTÉ took off *The Fugitive* to show us a film about the Easter Rising. We almost died, Shane and Mick and me, watching the GPO burn. The actor who played Dinny Byrne in *Glenroe* sang 'God Save Ireland', riddled with bullets while he shot his last few Brits.

We knelt down at night, like Patrick Pearse at his trial said that he had done as a child, and pledged our lives' blood for Ireland. It was all that we lived for. To grow up and die for Ireland. But meanwhile we played soccer in the back field where O'Brien couldn't find us and shout at how ungrateful we were:

"The chosen generation. Free at last to live in your own land. Yet turning your backs on Irish things. Living only for that English game."

The same game played by the children of my uncles and aunts who had been forced to leave Ireland before Westland Row became Pearse Street Station.

♣

Where was the first foreign station for Shane, Mick and me? Liverpool Street Station, London, in '81. That time we lost in Wembley. It was the first time we had been outside Ireland. We wound up in The Windmill Theatre. In the red-light land of Soho, of course.

We felt it was wild, never even dreaming of what somewhere like the Reeperbahn would be like, just a few miles from this Hamburg flat. Thankfully, I have a year or two left, Son, before you start wanting to explore the back lanes of that place.

But back then, in 1981, it was all new to us. Down below, in the seats of the Windmill Theatre, were five hundred Japanese tourists. Up on the balcony were two-hundred Irish fans on our best behaviour.

"Get them off you!"

A geezer in a suit kept walking on stage to say: "Gentlemen, if all noise does not cease the girls will not resume."

We all shut up for a while, until this girl came out dressed as a Roman slave and started off with the whip. Shane stood up.

"Jaysus, you wouldn't see the like of that in Garda Patrol!"

After that it was Holland in the '82 World Cup group campaign. That Two-All draw. We hit Amsterdam. Hippies with cobwebs growing out of their beards busking outside the station where our train stopped. The Flying Dutchman and The Bulldog pubs to our right. The red-light area and Chinatown to our left. We turned right for drugs and went left to smoke them.

Those were the flatland years. Shane finishing off his time with the ESB. Mick up in the factory in Finglas. Me thinking I was set up for life working in that new Japanese plant. We seemed to spend every night in Dublin being kicked out of pubs at closing time.

But that night in Amsterdam the pub was so jammed with Irish fans that we spilled out onto the street with our drinks. Next thing we knew, at two in the morning, all these police cars arrived.

"It feels just like home, lads," Shane said.

The police got out and – I am not joking – they pushed us *back into* the pub.

"I could get to like this country," Shane said. I wonder if he has, in the fifteen years that he has had to work there?

After that there were trips to see games in Belgium and Malta in '83. They became the only holidays we took. Saving money from our wages so that we never missed an away game. Never mind that Eoin Hand was the Irish manager back then and we never won a single thing. They were great years, great times to be young and alive.

No more trips to tiny stations in the bog now. It was about being out here in Europe, following the Irish team. Coming home like heroes to tell our work mates all about the places we had seen.

Then, in late 1984, when we played the Danes, Mick got his first taste of getting old. We hit Amsterdam again first and found the only snooker hall in the town. Mick sank a long red.

"It must be my birthday," he said. It was, too. He was twenty-six that day. He didn't mind losing his hair. It was losing the cheap travel rates that killed him. He did not have enough money for the full fare. Shane and myself went on to Denmark with a spare match ticket, leaving Mick to roll his own way to happiness in Amsterdam.

That trip to Denmark was when I saw the change in the Irish fans first. Three Kerry lads were trying to buy a ticket outside the ground, looking like they had just finished cutting hay back home. We gave them Mick's ticket for nothing. They told us about the time they had hitch-hiked to Malta from Kerry, when they were on the dole, to see Frank Stapleton get the winner. Their accents were so thick we found it hard to know what they were saying.

"How did you get here this time?" I asked them.

"We got the old bus, boy."

"The bus from Kerry?" I asked, in surprise.

"No. The bus from Berlin, boy. Sure, half of the factory is here."

And so they were too. Buses from Germany and Paris. Three buses from London. Irish lads who were working all over Europe mixing together with lads who had come from Dublin and Cork. A green army taking over the steps of the town hall.

I never knew until that night just how many Irish people were starting to have to leave Ireland to find work again. But that night — after the Danes beat us Three-Nil — listening to all the Irish workers telling their tales in the pubs scared the hell out of me. I don't know why, but it felt like the ground was starting to slide from under me. Yet I never knew just how soon Shane and Mick and me would also lose our jobs in Dublin. Just how soon we too would be forced to join them.

It was the same feeling I had that day in the 1970s when they brought Frank Stagg, the lone hunger striker, home to Mayo from the English jail where he died. I remember lines of Irish soldiers and tanks crossing the country. Taking his coffin to be buried under concrete like nuclear waste. Armed soldiers guarding his grave so that the IRA could not dig him back up and give him the funeral he had wanted.

Sitting in school that day, the three of us had listened to reports on the radio. We were remembering O'Brien's 1798 Pike. His talk about us growing up and fighting for a United Ireland. Dinny Byrne dying in black and white on TV just a few years before. The whole classroom could feel it. All of us walking home from school in silence. Nobody needed to say it. Some bastard somewhere along the line had been lying through their teeth to us. Someone somewhere.

You see, Son, we were meant to be the chosen ones. The generation who made sense of the last 700 years. Irishmen and Irishwomen, in the name of God and the dead generations. Living in our own land. With our own jobs. Our own homes that our fathers had worked to build for us. Can you understand me? All this having to leave Ireland for work was meant to have stopped before our time. Growing up in the 1970s, we were not raised to leave. We felt that we had a choice. But in the end we were wrong.

♣

I knew things were going to be different when I moved over here in 1986. I could even learn to cope with having to tell the police about any change in my address. But it was the main train station in Hamburg that still freaked me out. I remember in my first week in this city asking some man working there if I could get a train to Rome.

"No," he said, holding up one finger. "Not for one hour."

I used to come here in my first weeks in Hamburg just to read the timetables on the wall. Paris. Berlin. Bonn. Madrid. Every city across Europe could be reached by just crossing the platforms. I would remember those Irish town names laid out in painted stones in the flower beds beside the platforms and suddenly feel so cold. Like I had stepped outside of my old life.

Back in 1988 it was in the main Hamburg train station that I met Shane who had arrived from Holland, on the Saturday before the first match against England. Mick had flown in from Dublin the night before, as silent as ever. He handed me a bottle of duty-free whiskey and his holiday visa for the USA.

"Are you going to stay over there on the black?" I asked him.

He shrugged his shoulders. "Do I have a choice?"

He was right. I mean what else was there for him to do at home? He had held out on the dole in Dublin longer than either Shane or I had, since the factory he had worked in closed down.

Drinking with Mick on the Friday night we had been quiet. But Shane was his usual self. Jumping down off the train from Holland, slagging us. Ready for action:

"And it's hello to the German Bastard and The Quiet Man. Fingers on your buzzers, please. Here is your starter question in the quiz for ten points. Are we about to:

A) Collect and press wild flowers?

B) Add to our collection of odd barbed wire?

Or

C) Beat The Brits, the Godless Russians and the Dutch So-and-Sos I have to work with. While suffering brain death due to a large intake of drink and drugs."

"Stop the lights," we both said.

"Shag off," Shane said. "You got the right answer in C) and you have won yourself a free trip to Hamburg's Reeperbahn red light area. Lead the way."

But we didn't go there at first. We spent most of the afternoon hanging around the station. Watching the crowds get off the trains. The crew-cut Yanks with bags the size of a small estate in Finglas. Tourists from Canada always in red jackets with a Maple leaf on the back. The little French girls that would blow your mind away.

At last we took a train to the Reeperbahn. Slagging, driving each other crazy with football quiz questions. Mick had one that nearly killed us. To name the last three sets of brothers to play for Ireland at any level from youth up.

"Give us a break," I said. "I'm not a professor of history."

"No, they are all in the Irish squad, or should be," Mick told us.

That gave us the first one, it was easy enough.

"The O'Learys — Dave and Pearse," I said. "Then ... hang on, the Bradys, Liam and what's his name — his brother Ray, who played Under-21. But who else?" We were still racking our heads when the train reached the red light area.

"Hughton from Spurs," I said. "Chris Hughton had a brother who played Under-21. He broke his leg after, or was it somebody else's? For God's sake, Chris Hughton, of all the Irishmen ..."

We stopped laughing. No one said it but we all knew why I skipped him over. He was black and from London. I had fallen into the trap of the knockers. His mother had been from Limerick. She was forced to leave just the same as my own aunts and uncles. And just the same as the three of us now. Chris Hughton could have been a first cousin to any one of us.

Yet it had seemed so odd, back in the 1970s. When John Giles took over for his first game in charge, against Poland. I think Peter Thomas was the first English-born player. But he had played for Waterford since before the Vikings. Steve Highway followed. But it was a guy called Terry Mancaini who brought it home. That day in 1974 when Don Givens scored three goals against Russia. The odd moment when this bald man from London, playing his first game for Ireland, turned round during the playing of the Irish anthem, to whisper:

"Hey, this Russian anthem doesn't half go on, does it?"

It did not seem right back then. Like a party ruined by gate-crashers. Our own little club. Our local heroes from the same streets as us. More and more English-born players followed. New faces and accents to be suspicious of.

That was back then, when I still believed in that sense of what being Irish was. When they did not fit into my vision of Ireland. This was around the time my father came home with something extra in his wage packet. Uncle Sam was going home. The tax breaks and IDA grants wrung dry. The workers had a sit-in at the factory. I saw Da on the Nine O'clock News. Awkward in his Sunday suit. In a row of men behind the union official.

There was something chilling in that for me. My Da suddenly becoming a moment of history. On the TV screen, like Dinny Byrne shot to bits. Maybe I had always seen him too close up. But his face on the TV was like a map without name-places. After all that coming and going from Westland Row. All the years of his face growing old from chemical dust in that factory.

When he looked past the union man into the TV camera it was like he had at last reached his station to find it closed. Tumble-weed blowing down the platform. The signal box rusted. The very train tracks torn up.

Two months later, after the cars had returned from his grave, Shane and Mick and me sat up all night. Among the vast plates of sandwiches, drinking Guinness by the neck. I didn't weep. It was like cold water had entered my bloodstream. I doubted if I would ever be able to feel anything again.

♣

We set out for the England match on the Saturday night. Mick had got an An Óige Irish Youth Hostel card before he left. Mine was from the German Youth Hostel people. Shane's was from the Dutch one. We felt we were being clever in finding somewhere cheap to stay. But when we got to the game half the Irish fans were trying the same trick. Old lads who could claim the free travel. Women who would only see forty again on the front of a Finglas bus. They had all suddenly become International Youth Hostel members.

I have told you all about the England match before now. John Aldridge flicking it on to Ray Houghton's head. Packy Bonner's saves. My nerves in bits. After Ireland won the game One-Nil and the Irish team had finally left the pitch, we walked singing from the ground. To face rows of riot police with dogs. Shane turned to us.

"Time to leave this town, boys."

We found a small bar above the city. Down below us the fag end of the British Empire, fed on white bread and the *News of the World*, could run riot. All we wanted to do was sit there and enjoy it. A coming of age.

"I wonder what Dublin is like?" Shane said. "All car horns hooting and pubs packed I suppose."

Toners Bar in Baggot Street. The Hill pub. The Hut pub near Dalymount. I could imagine them all and yet … You know when you dream of something which is so real that when you awaken you still want to believe it was there. Even when you know it is gone.

Shane went silent. We would never know now what Dublin was like that night. Because even if we went back and those pubs had not changed, we would have found that we had changed. And I knew, and I think Shane knew, that now when we said '*us*', we were no longer thinking about the people in those Dublin pubs. But of the army of Irish fans from all over Europe singing in every bar and hotel in the city below us that night.

We drank now in stunned silence. I knew that we were remembering the same things. Winter evenings in the shed in Dalymount Park with people climbing up onto the roof for a better view of the game. Landsdowne Road in the years after. Liam Brady's goal against France, that little jinking run. Frank Stapleton's two against Spain in 1982. All the flats with cheap televisions where we would gather to scream our heads off at the TV set for away games we could not get to. The killer blow of that Belgium goal minutes away from the final whistle. Just when Eoin Hand was about to make the impossible dream of getting us into the World Cup finals a reality.

But it wasn't really football we were thinking about anymore. It was something else. Something we had lost, that we had hardly even been aware we'd had. That dream of finally getting into some big finals and of coming home to Dublin with stories to tell people. There is no greater feeling than the feel of going home, of having a home to go back to.

"Shag it," Shane said, quietly to himself. "Shag it."

You see, there would be no one for Shane to tell when he got back to Holland. No one in Hamburg for me. Oh, German people in work you could talk to about the game. But not the feel of it. Not the sense of being part of that event.

Late in the evening, two England fans came into the bar. Harmless, sad-looking wasters, with skinhead haircuts and Union Jack tattoos. Terrified to be out alone. They looked at us in fear, wondering if they would be served. Shane called them over.

"Two beers for our friends. The poor wee pets. Sit down here, good *surs*."

Sur is an Irish word for lice, *Pet* is the Spanish word for fart. They looked down on us, while being slagged in three languages. We brought them beer and waited. We knew they could not hold out long. It was the third beer before they got started.

"I can't believe it. I mean, England beaten by our own second team."

"Yeah, I believe Ray Houghton went through Dublin on a bus once."

"What do you call five men from England, three Blacks, a Scot, an ape and a frog? The Irish soccer team."

We let them talk away, getting more cocky and loud with each drink. Not aware that even the barman was breaking up laughing at the way we were secretly making fun of them. They left after a while. Shuffling out into the night. Hanging on to the rock of Gibraltar by their fingertips.

"I don't mind those fools mocking the team," Shane said after a while. "It's the ones at home that piss me off."

Home? Where the hell was home for us anymore?

♣

After crossing Germany again for the draw with Russia, we went on to the town of Gelsenkirchen to play the Dutch. There was no hostel there. The only one we could find was far out in the country. There was only one other Irish fan staying there, so they put us in with him. He was seventeen, just after doing his Leaving Cert.

"I am staying over here," he said. "After the games are over. I'll try and find some work."

The hostel was full of young Germans. Happy, loud and shrill. Rising at six o'clock to play games outside our window. Mick sat on the step, nursing his hangover, looking at them.

"Have them little bastards no traffic to play in?" he asked.

But being back among Germans sobered me up. That afternoon I went down to use the public phone. Lots of young Germans crowded around the Coke machine, screaming. I phoned your mother in Hamburg. The click on the line. Her German voice bringing my new life back to me. I could not believe her news.

"Are you sure?" I asked. "Yes, I know. What can I say? Of course I am happy. Just surprised. You said it might take months after you coming off the pill … Yes, I will be back in Hamburg tomorrow night. Alone if we lose. Or with the lads for the semi-final if we draw. Yes, with the lads. You will like them. It is great news … I love you too."

I went back up. Through the young German voices. I said nothing about the phone call to the lads. I could not tell them. They knew that I was living with a German girl. But nothing about our plans. But I knew at once that you would be a boy. Your high Irish cheekbones and raven black hair, standing out from all the German faces when I would bring you to school.

Would you believe me, I wondered, when I tried to tell you about O'Brien. About the three of us kicking a ball around that dirty concrete schoolyard in Dublin.

But as I sat on the steps of that hostel in the back of nowhere, I seemed to be on the edge of two worlds. Neither the Dublin I had come from, nor the Hamburg I had to go back to felt real anymore. Even the news about you didn't sink in. There was just this tension in the pit of my stomach that I knew would not stop until the final whistle blew in that game against the Dutch.

♣

We dressed in silence on the morning of the game. We wore the same clothes as at the other games. We looked at each other, not knowing where would we sleep that night. In Munich if we beat the Dutch and got into the first semi-final. In Hamburg, together for the other semi-final, if we drew with the Dutch. And if we lost? Nobody wanted to even think about that.

"I never felt this sick before a game," Mick said.

We were always nervous before a game, but I knew this was different from ever before. This was no longer just about a football match. No longer just how long the Irish team could stay in Germany. It was about how much longer we three could stay together, pretending that our lives were the same. That we were still part of the Ireland of our youth.

We got to the ground. Made it past the skinheads and the loose stones. Saw the vast Dutch crowd in a blaze of orange on three sides on the ground. We all packed into one corner behind Packy Bonner's goal.

There were faces we knew from the first two games. Faces from Dublin. Faces we had never seen before. All together in one wave of green. And when the game started we screamed and shouted and sang our hearts out for the lads.

For Packy Bonner and Paul McGrath, running himself into the ground. For Frank Stapleton, suddenly old and making us old. Holding up the ball. Using up those few extra seconds. Paul McGrath rose at the far post and we rose with him, our arms out, flags flying, dreaming, praying. We watched the ball spin off the Dutch post. Jesus, how close could we get?

Would this game ever end? My mouth was dry. My legs trembling. My heart frightened me. An old lad beside me tried to sit on the ground, no longer able to bear it. All around us forty-five thousand Dutch roared their team forward. Drowning out our voices. How could we make ourselves heard? It was like throwing stones into the sea.

"Sing your heart out,
Sing your heart out,
Sing your heart out for the lads.
Ireland! Ireland! Ireland!"

Could the lads hear us? Did they know we were with them? Half-time came and still we lived in hope. We sat on the steps, our faces white. Trying to suck in deep breaths. How could we ever get through another forty-five minutes in this heat?

The lads were wrecked. You could see it in them in the second half. The Dutch passing it around, making them run for each ball. I closed my eyes and sat down, suddenly unable to watch anymore.

I opened them again as the shout went up. Forty-five thousand Dutch voices, filling up my head. Banging off my skull. The most lucky of goals, mis-hit. Leaving Packy with no chance. The flag went up for off-side. Then it was put down again. The Dutch goal was allowed. Shane's hand touched my shoulder.

"It's over," he said, "over."

I stood up amongst the silent men and women, their faces white, and I raised my hands.

"Ireland!" I screamed. "Ireland! Ireland!" I had six minutes of my old life to go. Six minutes more to cheat time. The crowd joined in with me. Every one of them. From Dublin and Cork. From London and all over Europe. And suddenly I knew this was the only country I still owned. Those eleven men in green shirts, half of whom were born abroad.

Shane and Mick stood firm at my right and left shoulders. I knew they were thinking too of the long train journeys ahead. The tunnel was being pulled out for the end of the match. Men gathering down on the touch-line. We lifted our voices in that wall of noise, one last time to urge the lads on.

"Ireland! Ireland! Ireland!"

And then the final whistle blew. I lowered my head feeling suddenly old. The players sank down, knees pressed into the grass, as the Dutch jumped up and down. When I looked around after a few minutes, none of us were moving as the Dutch fans filed away, more relieved than happy.

And when the Dutch were gone, we stayed on, to a man and a woman. Thirteen thousand of us, cheering, applauding. Chanting out the players' names. Letting them know how proud we felt. I thought of my father's battered travel bag. Of O'Brien drilling us behind that 1798 pike. The teachers who came after him hammering *Peig* into us. The masked men blowing limbs off shoppers in my name.

You know, all my life it seemed to me that somebody somewhere was always trying to tell me what Ireland I belonged in. But I only belonged there with those fans. I raised my hands and clapped, having finally, in my last moments with Shane and Mick, found the only Ireland whose name I can sing. Given to me by eleven men dressed in green. And the only Ireland I can pass on to you, my son, as you carry my name in a foreign land.

I thought of my uncles and my aunts scattered across England and the USA. Of every generation shipped off like beef by the hoof. And at that moment it seemed to me that they had found a voice at last. That all those English-born players were playing for all the Irish mothers and father written out of history. And I knew that they were playing for you too, my son. And for Shane and Mick's children, who would grow up with foreign accents and Irish faces, confused by their fathers' lives.

All thirteen thousand of us stood in that ground, for fifteen or twenty minutes after the last player had gone. After Ray Houghton had come back out, sadly waving an Irish flag. After Jack Charlton had come back out also to stand and look up in wonder at us.

Coffin ships. The decks of cattle boats. The queues at airports. We were not a chosen generation any longer. We had just been a hiccup. A small stutter in the system. Thirteen thousand of us stood as one on that German terrace, before scattering back towards Ireland and out like a river bursting its banks. Heading back to every corner of Europe.

I did not need to look at Shane or Mick. We all knew that a part of our lives was over forever. We had always gone back home together before. Years spent in a limbo of youth. With poker games and parties in bedsits. With football in Fairview Park on Sunday mornings before the pubs opened. Walking out the long road to Rathmines on Saturday nights with six packs and dope and a sense that we belonged so deep inside us that we didn't even know it was there until we lost it.

"Italy, 1990 lads," Shane said, "we'll be there."

But we knew that we wouldn't be there, even if Ireland got there. We knew that our new lives were too far apart. Jesus, we all felt so old suddenly.

"We did it," Shane said. "The first time ever. We were a part of it."

I can still see us, like in a photograph, on that platform. Twenty-eight years of age. One life behind us. Another ahead. Laughing together. Proud.

Friends like I would never really have friends again. We shook hands and walked away from each other for the last time. You were a year-and-a-half-old when Ireland played in the World Cup in Italy. I watched the games on TV. But I had more important things on my mind. Shane did not go either. He was getting married in Holland at the time. He wanted me to be his best man. But you got sick on the week of his wedding and I had to stay here instead.

I don't know if Mick ever came back from America. He never wrote. Letters and writing were not his thing. I suppose he saw the games in America, four years later, when we beat Italy in the World Cup and the bloody Dutch knocked us out again. But I may never know what happened to him. Your sister was born that year. There was no way I could go off to watch football in the USA.

It is hard enough to find the money to go back to Ireland every two years. And, in truth, there are less and less people I want to see there. Dublin is full of jobs now, they say, with factories crying out for workers. But our roots are here now, in Germany. Your mother would never fit in. She has her mother and father here still and I have nobody like that in Dublin. Maybe I don't think that I could ever trust Ireland not to go bust again. Still, sometimes I think of talking your mother into packing up and trying to start afresh again in Dublin. But we could never afford a house there now. And, besides, I don't have what lured my father home — I have no family waiting there.

I've made a life for us in Germany, for better or worse. You can never go back. You can only go forward. All the same, with your golden feet and dribbling skill, you need not think that you will ever play for Germany. One day it will be an Irish shirt you will pull on. You will stand in Dublin to look at the crowd and say to yourself in German, "This is for my father."

Because it was the thought of you that made me turn my back on my native land, which had already turned its back on me. That night, after I left Shane and Mick, I walked down to a platform and boarded the train back to Hamburg alone. When the ticket inspector came in, he saw my Ireland scarf and nodded with a new respect.

I remembered my father in carriages like that. Always coming home to his son in Ireland. But when I closed my eyes the Ireland I saw wasn't the streets I had known as a child or the country fields that he had grown in. I saw thirteen-thousand sets of hands moving as one. United by pride.

I knew your mother would still be waiting up. With you, my child, my future, like a tiny pearl growing inside her.

"Come on train," I said, "faster, faster, take me home to her and him."

The lights of lots of German towns spread out while the train raced on. And all the way back here to Hamburg it wasn't the wheels that were singing. But the very web of train tracks, carrying all thirteen thousand of us away from there. Casting us like seed all over Europe. Those train lines were chanting ...

"Olé, Olé, Olé, Olé, Ireland, Ireland!
Olé, Olé, Olé, Olé, Ireland, Ireland!"

A POET'S NOTEBOOK

This poem was written after I found an old set of records at home. Being used to CDs, my kids thought they were something from the dark ages.

I put on a Tom Waits record that I had last heard over ten years ago. It was in the small flat of a friend of mine in Ranelagh, whom I used to call over to on a Saturday night.

We would wander downtown to meet friends in different bars and maybe wind up playing poker for half the night in some flat. Perhaps some of us would crash out on the floor, or else I might walk out to Finglas in the dawn. Taxi fares were well beyond my reach.

The poem is about remembering that freedom of my early twenties and those summer evenings of youth when time seems to stretch out forever before you.

Martha

I found the box of old albums,
Blew dust off a disused needle,

Tom Waits began to sing 'Martha'.
Once again I was twenty-four,

The pull of hash and tobacco,
Cheap white wine at my elbow

At the window of your bedsit
In the dust-filled August light.

A needle bobbing over warped vinyl
One final time before we stroll

Down to bars where friends gather.
Decks to be shuffled, numbers rolled,

Blankets bagged on some dawn-lit floor.
Our lives are just waiting to occur

As we linger in the infinity it takes
For the voice of Tom Waits to fade.

Some years ago I was chairman of a company called Music Base. It was set up to give free advice to young musicians and make sure they were not ripped off by sharks in the music business. For some reason the powers-that-be were not too happy with this. Eventually for funding reasons we had to close down.

A quiet, shy Irishman dying in a London hospital sometimes phoned the switchboard, just for someone to talk to. He was Rory Gallagher, the wonderful guitar-player who was such a huge figure in my childhood.

When he died, we opened a book in the office where the public could sign or write something in memory of him. This poem, written on the day he died, is what I wrote. It's set around the time when I was finishing school in the 1970s. At a certain point of every party back then, Rory Gallagher's music would be played.

i.m. Rory Gallagher

There came a time on those summer nights
    When a free house had been found,
And a cheap stereo rigged with strobe lights
    That froze each moment in your mind.

You just knew when the crowd had waned
    And the wasters had long gone
That soon the wised-up boys who remained
    Would put Rory Gallagher on.

I was born at home in Finglas. I now live in Drumcondra. My house in Drumcondra is like a small version of the house in Finglas in terms of layout. So much so that sometimes when I look out the bathroom window in Drumcondra I half expect to see the long gardens of Finglas Park.

This poem explores the idea that perhaps there is only ever one place we can call home. Even now, some mornings when I wake, I still half-expect to find myself back there.

The poem was written — like many of my poems — on the back of an envelope while walking my dog at night. Sometimes as you walk words just come to you. I had to tie the dog to the gate of a big house to have my hands free to write the poem. The owner came out and threatened to call the police. He thought I was a robber.

Perhaps all poets at night get mistaken for robbers. But I wonder how many robbers get mistaken for poets?

Wherever You Woke

There only ever was one street,
    One back garden, one bedroom:
Wherever you woke you woke beneath

    The ceiling where you were born,
For the briefest half-conscious second
    An eyelid's flutter from home.

I was almost forty before I knew that I'd had an uncle I never heard of. He died in great pain in Green Street in Wexford at the age of seventeen.

Child deaths in those years and right up into the 1950s were common. Most Irish families have children who died and never got to leave a mark, or have children of their own to follow after them.

I wanted to write a very stark poem in memory of those forgotten people.

Lines for an Unknown Uncle

(i.m. Francis Bolger, died 3rd June, 1928, aged 17.)

No son or granddaughter to remember:
　　No trace of your seventeen years left,
Except in the mind of a younger brother

　　Sent out onto the street to wait,
While you screamed in the height of fever
　　For someone to finish you with an axe.

My first job was working in a factory in Finglas. I wrote a book of poems, based on the lives of people I met there or around the streets at that time. It was called Finglas Lilies.

At that time nobody wrote about the Dublin life I knew. I was very concerned to carefully put down names like Finglas and Ballymun in the poems and say that these places and these lives existed and deserved to be recorded.

Finglas Lilies

I: The party, June 1977

A girl lies in the grass,
Beyond the lights of houses,
    As dew soaks into her back.

    Flocks of leaves swarm
Above them like water lilies
    Over a sunken garden.

    Dawn forms like silver stubble:
An unshaven morning surfaces,
    Jaded and looking for trouble.

    Her hair feels like seaweed,
Salty and drenched to touch.
    Like the cry of clubbed seals,

    Her scared cry pushes them apart,
As he withdraws from her too late
    And dreams seep into the grass.

II: London, Autumn 1977

A tiny flat in West London,
　They live on frozen food,
Make friends across the landing.

At night she often cries.
　They make love softly
For fear of harming the child

Developing like a negative
　In the pit of her stomach.
They finally call her relatives.

On the night crossing Dublin rose
　Like a curtain over a window
With thousands of bullet holes.

III: Finglas, 1979

Steel wings at dawn sting like a wasp,
   In this factory where men curse
And rust grows like hair on a corpse.

She's off to work as he finishes night shift.
   Today is their child's first birthday,
They'll put his name on the housing list.

Taking a chair he sits in the garden,
   Smoking Moroccan dope and tripping,
The housing estate keeps disappearing.

He feels himself at the bottom of a pond,
   Floating below rows of water lilies
With new names like Finglas and Ballymun.

As a writer with two small children, I use different rooms around the city as places where I can try to find the space and quiet to write in the daytime. Some years ago I found myself renting a room in Dorset Street over an archway which led down a lane.

On the day I left the room I decided to walk down the lane and see where it led. I suddenly found myself back at the Temple Street Children's Hospital, outside the same door that I used to enter with my mother. As a child I had very bad speech problems. Nobody could understand a word I said and I was regarded at school as a bit of a dunce.

My mother took me to speech therapy there. She died when I was ten. Many of my last memories of her are of us sitting in the waiting room there, before my lessons. She worried greatly about me. The speech therapist told her that, behind my speech problems, I was "a bright penny", but my mother never lived to see any proof of that.

As I stood there, almost thirty years later, watching another mother and child leave the same building, I wrote the first draft of this poem on an old piece of paper I found lying on the roadway.

Temple Street Children's Hospital

I

This is your territory, I brought you here:
Shoddy tenement windows where washing flaps,
Crumbling lanes where cars get broken for parts.

There is an archway beneath which we passed –
Like the one above which you shared a flat
With your sisters up from Monaghan for work

In a war-becalmed Dublin. Surely you must once
Have gazed up, puzzled by how the years since
Had landed you here with a son, a stuttering misfit,

Unable to say the most simple of words,
A bright penny whose cloud you'd never see lift
As you fretted, unaware of how close death hovered.

The speech therapist's office had fancy toys and books
And a special mirror which allowed me to be watched.
The waiting room contained a large white clock

Which ticked off the final hours we spent alone,
Gazing down at a garden where I longed to walk,
Trapped indoors by the shame of my garbled tongue.

II

I stand outside that hospital in Nerney's Court,
At Kelly's Row where a blacksmith once worked,

And no logic can explain why you feel this close,
Why I see us in the mother and child who pass,

Or how, as I age, I slowly become your son,
Gazing through your eyes with incomprehension.

I was too young to have known you, so it makes no sense
That every passing year only deepens your absence.

Some years ago a very old friend of mine told me how her son, after his death, seemed able to send her various messages that he was okay, and that it was time to let go. This very short poem is about the same thing.

Wishbone

Do not be afraid, my oldest friend,
　　To send a sign that you are gone:
　　　　In the sadness after your funeral

　　　　Visit me unexpectedly some morning,
　　Your face behind mine in a mirror
Glimpsed for an instant, startlingly young.

From being a son myself and writing about that, I now find myself a father. People think that a poet will be so moved by the birth of his or her children that they will write a poem for on the spot.

But, like any parent, I was too engaged in the here-and-now wonder and sheer work of having a new-born child to have time to mark it in verse.

It was only later, doing quite ordinary things, that the magic of being a father worked its way into my poems. This is one of three poems that I wrote for my sons. They mark simple things that their mother and I do with them, like collecting chestnuts or, in this case, just walking in the park.

Being with a young child you see everything through new eyes, filled with the wonder they have in discovering the world.

Walking in Spring With My Sons

Let us search for tractors and motorbikes,
Let the evening be bewitched with promise,
The man who chains the gates of the park
A distant sandman not to be glimpsed yet.

And let me share your eyes as we look
For birds nesting in sycamore and ash;
Let your fingers nestle in my palms
As you point in wonder at trailers and trucks,

And we stride with such tremendous purpose
After our shadows stretching along the path.

Like most Dublin boys I began playing football on the street at the age of five. Now, thirty-five years later, my ankles may be clapped out, my back wrecked and a snail could overtake me, but I still find myself playing every Friday night.

This poem was written on the eve of my 40th birthday, a cold night of heavy rain when all the young men who play never showed up. The older lads did however, knowing that they should have stopped playing years ago and soon will have to. But for now they were still determined to enjoy every last minute of every last game.

Approaching Forty

The young men fall off on nights like this:
Nobody shows at first in the teeming hail
As floodlights illuminate the vacant pitch.
Slowly a handful of cars start to show.
Drivers stare out at the January gale
Then exchange looks through their windows.

Nobody in their right mind would play football
On a night when not even dogs would stir,
But a car door opens and slagging voices call.
Men clamber out with strapped ankles and bad backs
To stretch, warm up, laugh at the downpour,
Knowing they won't always enjoy Fridays like that.

ALSO IN THE SERIES:

SAD SONG by Vincent Banville

John Blaine is a private detective, who walks Dublin's mean streets. He is tough and smart, but unlucky in love — his wife has just left him. Hired to bring home a straying daughter, he takes the girl's side against her rich father, and suffers for it.

Gripping, funny and stripped to the bone, *Sad Song* is a short novel that packs a punch like a fist in a velvet glove ...

NOT JUST FOR CHRISTMAS by Roddy Doyle

Danny Murphy is going to meet his brother, Jimmy. They haven't seen each other in over twenty years. On the way to the meeting, Danny remembers the good times and the bad times, the fun and the fights — and the one big row that drove them apart. Will they fight again or will they become the friends they used to be? Danny doesn't know.

MAGGIE'S STORY by Sheila O'Flanagan

Maggie is forty-three years old and looking for romance. She loves her husband, Dan, but his idea of romance is a couple of drinks at the local and an early night at home.
Her children think she's too old to care. And she's beginning to wonder if life has passed her by. But a

chance meeting changes all that, and now Maggie faces
tough decisions. Can she put the spark back into her
marriage, or would she be better off calling it a day?
And who is more important?
Her husband? Her children?
Or herself?

JESUS AND BILLY ARE OFF TO BARCELONA
by Deirdre Purcell

Billy is an average-looking sixteen-year-old who lives
in an ordinary Dublin estate on the northside of the city.
Jesus, on the other hand, is a beautiful boy with
Continental manners, from the poshest part of
Barcelona. He travels from Spain to live with Billy's
family for three weeks one summer. The plan is that at
the end of the holiday, Billy will go back with Jesus on
a return visit. However, no one should make plans ...

RIPPLES by Patricia Scanlan

The McHughs' marriage is on the rocks.
Daughter Ciara worries that her mother and father are
going to divorce. Lillian, Ciara's Gran, is worried too.
She has a nice life now, since her bullying husband
died. This could all change. Meanwhile, Brenda
Johnston is very happy. She has a lot to gain if the
McHughs divorce. Or has she?
And Mike and Kathy Stuart, the McHughs' best friends,
are beginning to wonder if the friendship can survive.
Then, one awful night, everything changes ...

ORDER FORM

___ *Sad Song* by Vincent Banville
    ISBN: 1 902602 18 8, £4.99
___ *In High Germany* by Dermot Bolger
    ISBN: 1 902602 14 5, £4.99
___ *Not Just for Christmas* by Roddy Doyle
    ISBN: 1 902602 15 3, £4.99
___ *Maggie's Story* by Sheila O'Flanagan
    ISBN: 1 902602 17 X, £4.99
___ *Jesus and Billy Are Off to Barcelona* by Deirdre Purcell
    ISBN: 1 902602 13 1, £4.99
___ *Ripples* by Patricia Scanlan
    ISBN: 1 902602 13 7, £4.99

TRADE ORDERS TO:
CMD, 55A Spruce Avenue,
Stillorgan Industrial Park, Blackrock, Co Dublin, Ireland.
Tel. (+353 1) 294 2560
Fax. (+353 1) 294 2564

EDUCATIONAL AND PERSONAL ORDERS TO:
New Island Books, 2 Brookside, Dundrum Road,
Dundrum, Dublin 14, Ireland.
Tel: (+353 1) 298 9937/298 3411
Fax: (+353 1) 298 2783
E-Mail: nibsales@brookside.iol.ie
Please include a cheque or postal order for the amount
payable to New Island Books,
plus £2 for post and packaging.